Snow White Desire

~o~

Reverse Harem Fairy Tales

Book 6

TIMEA TOKES

ISBN: 9798712934355

DEDICATION

To all my lovely readers out there. Remember, no matter what your dreams are (naughty or not), you have everything you need to make them come true.

If you love my writing style, please check out my other titles on Amazon, and follow me on my blog & website for a FREE pdf copy of Squirm Under My Watch, FREE Audiobooks, and other goodies, to say a personal thank you to you all.

I am also hosting a monthly signed paperback giveaway, with at least 2 winners each month. So, please stay tuned, and share the love that's deep inside all of you.

Thank you!

www.timeatokes.com

ACKNOWLEDGMENTS

Chapter 1

~o~

They chased me before, although that time their intentions weren't to kill me. Another arrow whizzes past my left ear, and I barely escape its deadly poison this time. I duck the last second, and the tip lodges into a tree branch inches above my head, the breeze it creates lifting the edges of my hair.

A branch scrapes my upper arm, drawing blood, but I don't feel the pain from the adrenaline that's coursing through my veins. My skin tingles and my heart skips a beat as realisation dawns: I'm not going to survive tonight. But, instead of being scared or upset, all I feel is anger and disappointment.

Time slows to a halt as I watch the dark green liquid drip to the ground, searing it black, destroying all living things in its wake. And then I'm running again, my feet making an awful lot of noise while crunching into the fallen leaves. They crumble underneath my weight, making me wonder just how fragile life truly is.

It isn't the first time I'm overwhelmed by such gloomy thoughts, either. My mother was taken away from me before I could get to know her. I have a few vague memories, but I rather sense her than remember her, really, as she died when I was a babe. A year ago, my father followed her, obtaining a deadly wound during one of his hunting trips. The boar was found and killed, but my heart never healed.

Death has always been part of my life, whether I liked it or not. And so has been the evil queen, the woman who caused my father's early demise, and who is trying to ensure I don't see another day. She sent the best of the best to hunt me down. There are no more arrows, just the distant sound of boots destroying the innocent leaves.

I attempt a glance back, only to stumble. As I reach for a branch to steady myself, it breaks and I nearly end up rolling down a path into certain death. part of me even considers the possibility that I *should*, when the sound of the hunters reaches me once more, urging me to carry on.

I know they are toying with me. They are hunters. This is what they do. I am prey now, thanks to the evil queen. That arrow didn't miss me by accident. They are luring me deeper into the woods, and there is nothing I can do about it.

If I turn back and face them, I sign my own death warrant, and if I keep running, I will be consumed by the animals they should be hunting instead of me. Still, I would pick the animals and monsters any day over the men who are chasing me. And to think that I used to know them... I used to trust them and I used to trust her.

And those were the biggest mistakes of my life.

With heart plummeting in my chest, I pick up the pace, even though my legs are aching, and my feet are covered in cuts and bruises from the rough brush. I feel bad for the nature I destroy, but it's another thing I can't do much about. Trying to find some form of comfort, I gently twist the silver ring around my finger, and it warms up instantly, melting my insides.

I didn't have time or a chance to put my shoes on. I'm practically naked, too, barely covered by a now half-torn nightgown. All I took was the ring my mother left for me as part of my inheritance. As to the other part, well...

My father's second wife is sitting on the throne, torturing the people of our lands. A painful memory tears at my chest, but I push it away. I can't afford to be distracted by emotions right now. I tried to fight her, but I can't afford to fight her now.

Not while I'm running for my life.

I need to change course, because a massive oak is blocking my way. I don't have time to think; I turn left where the trees are thicker and the light is scarce. It is rumoured that beasts roam these woods, not just simple wolves and bears. But I need to take that risk.

I can hear the hunters. I can smell the musky aroma of their leather jackets, and I can feel their hot breath at the nape of my neck. I know they are not that close, but they aren't far behind, either. Even though I'm not sure they brought the royal hounds, these hunters are deadly either way. They shoot *then* ask questions, and there is a prize on my head. A hefty prize that would make everyone wealthy as the queen herself.

Whether I'm captured dead or alive is irrelevant...

I let out a colourful curse when I trip in a semi-hidden branch, beginning to feel like even the woods don't want me to leave here alive. But then again, why would they? Nobody ever returned, except for the hunters. I don't know why they don't just leave me here. I'm pretty sure this enchanted (or more likely cursed) forest would do the job for them.

Because I'm preoccupied by my thoughts, I don't see the next arrow, neither do I expect the excruciating pain that courses through my body when it pierces my skin just below my left shoulder. I look at the wound, feeling nauseous. Fighting the poison is out of the question, I know that and so are any attempts to pull the arrow out. It's getting dark and cold, and my prospects aren't too rosy.

All I can do is find cover for the night, so they only find me when I'm dead.

I've come to terms with my fate. I know I don't have much time left on this earth, but even so, whatever gruesome tortures are awaiting me, I am not going back. I simply can't face the evil queen after what happened. She did something to me that I will never forget, and I did something myself that I will never forgive.

The woods are helpful, after all: there is a cave in front of me, but it could also be that I'm so far gone that I'm hallucinating. I think I can even hear my mother's voice, singing my favourite lullaby - of course, it was my father who sang it for me when I was little, his voice resembling a broken harp rather than the voice of my mother. What I remember of it anyway.

I never blamed him though. He always tried his best to cheer me up, or provide a shoulder to cry on. I will never forget what he did for me, even though we have grown distant since he met his new love. I shake my head. I can't let myself be distracted again.

The world is spinning by the time I climb up the steep hill that leads to the cave, but once inside, the darkness envelopes me like a thick blanket. I no longer feel the cold, nor do I hear the hunters. They are still behind me though, I can feel it.

With a sigh, I step further inside, half-expecting a bear or a beast to jump out me and devour what's left of my soul, but the cave is empty and cosy as a mother's arms. It doesn't take me long to find a dry spot and put my wary head to rest. I fall asleep playing with the silver band of the ring, holding it close to my heart.

My mother's singing is the last thing I hear before darkness takes over.

~o~

Chapter 2

~o~

I know I'm dreaming, or rather drifting away, my life force dissipating, but I just can't make myself end the dream. I have experienced this many times before, although it has never been so intense. There were always rumours in the kingdom that certain witches possessed the ability to control their (and other people's) dreams, but as I didn't possess any magical powers, I kept this a secret.

Now I'm running in the woods once again, although it's daytime and the woods are different. It takes me a moment to recognise the place, but when I do, a tear escapes from the corner of my eye, rolling down my cheek. I raise a hand to wipe it off, only to notice that I am much younger in this dream than in reality.

A sad smile plays at my lips when I hear the familiar voice from behind me:

"Are you alright, sweetheart?"

I turn around as quickly as I can, running to my father. He envelopes me in his arms, his huge form towering over me. But then again, I am but a child.

"I'm fine, father. It's just a little scratch."

He smiles down at me knowingly, taking my hand in his. I wince in pain, pulling away. I glance down at my hand with a frown, raising an eyebrow at the deep cut that runs across my palm. My cheeks must loose their colour, too, because my dad shakes his head, then tears a piece off from the sleeve of his shirt, gently bandaging the wound.

"There you go. Adrena, I hope you know that you don't need to act brave and strong when you are with me. I understand."

I shake my head, sending charcoal tendrils flying around my face, a ten-year-old's determination reflected in my eyes.

"No, daddy, I do. I need to stay strong for you."

My father looks at me for a long moment, then lets out a sigh, tucking a lock behind my ear.

"No, sweetheart, that's my duty. Promise you will take care of yourself?"

I know he wants to add that I should be nicer to Clarise, too, and I'm really trying, but she isn't making it too easy. I simply nod, the pain in my palm dulling a little. My father shakes his head, as if not believing me.

"Listen, darling, I need to leave you for a while. I want to make sure you are going to be okay."

His words scare me a little, but I don't show it. I am used to him being away, and even though there is something sad in his tone, I assume it's due to the fact that he wants to stay.

"I will be fine. I promise."

He nods again, his hand lingering on my hair. Then he pulls me into another bear hug, and I only wince a little when his stubble grazes the wound on my palm.

Suddenly, he pulls away, and produces a tiny trinket box from his pocket. He pops the lid open and I study the gorgeous ring with admiration, a memory trying to come to the surface, but I am unable to grasp it.

"Here, I want you to have this. It was your mother's."

I gasp at him, and his eyes mist over with emotion. He places the ring onto my palm, and it feels warm. A soothing calm washes over me and I close my fist around the silver band, knowing too well that I will spend countless hours examining the pale blue stones.

"Thank you, father. You don't know how much this means to me..."

He smiles down at me.

"I loved her more than anything, you know. Up until the day you arrived, she was my everything."

He trails off, his mind stuck in the past, and part of me wishes I could see her through his eyes. All the stories of her beauty, kindness and adventurous nature make me feel like I know her, but it isn't enough. It can never be enough, and it can never erase the sleepless nights I spent weeping into my pillow.

"I know. Tell me how you met. Please?"

He lets out a soft laugh, wiping at his eyes with his big hands.

"Are you sure you aren't getting bored of the story yet? You've heard it at least a thousand times."

I shake my head, settling down into the grass, patting it beside me. He sits down gingerly.

"Never. Every time is like the first."

He looks away, his eyes distant once again.

"Yes, I guess it is."

And with that, he begins the magical story I heard so many times, and yet, every single time it makes my heart flutter. Suddenly, the gloomy day isn't so gloomy after all, and my soul is filled with hopes for the future. I want to find someone who would love me the way my father loved my mother. Even though she wasn't his only queen, she will always be a part of his soul.

~o~

Chapter 3

~o~

Suddenly, the dream changes, and yet again, it captivates me with the bittersweet beauty of the memory. They do say that the best and worst moments of your life flash before your eyes moments before you exhale your last breath, so I embrace the next scene with an open heart and mind.

The woods are the same, but my father has disappeared. I'm running yet again, breathless and giggling, cheeks flushed with heat. The sun is warm on my skin, the gentle wind playing with my hair. They are after me and I laugh, hiding behind the trunk of a massive oak tree, its leaves tickling the back of my neck.

I try to hold my breath and blend in, but it's no use: they find me, their eyes roaming my body.

"Got you."

Cain says in a low voice that resembles a predator's growl, his green eyes filled with hunger. I gulp down my sudden fear, looking over his gorgeous body. The loose linen shirt doesn't do his muscles any justice, but the tight leather trousers, on the other hand, make me blush with their delicious promise. His long wavy light brown hair is being picked up by the wind, giving him a mysterious aura.

I smile at him coyly, pushing myself away from the tree trunk, only to fall back against it when he places a hand on each side of my shoulders, trapping me.

"Where do you think you are going?"

Basil joins in from behind him, his gorgeous chocolate eyes melting my insides. I open my mouth to reply, and Cain captures it for a brief, yet breath-taking kiss, stating his claim. I groan into his mouth, then bite and suck on his lower lip, knowing how much he likes that, and the aroused growl that leaves his lips confirms my suspicion: he wants me again. I smile against his lips and he pushes me deeper into the tree, the barks digging into my back.

"Easy there, Cain. Leave us some, would you?"

That was Dorran, the third hunter that my stepmother hired to 'entertain' me. I found it weird at first, but she said it was necessary. One day I would marry a prince, and he would expect me to be experienced in the matters of love. According to her, the bolder I become, the better.

I blush at the thought, now knowing too well what she meant. I am a fast learner, and her hunters are eager to teach me every trick in the books. Some of the things scare me though, so I asked them to go easy on me.

Stepmother expects a report every night, and a shiver runs through me when I recall the delicious punishment I receive when I don't obey or on days when I don't learn enough. Those days, she takes matters into her own hands, teaching me of ways the hunter can't. She claims that to know how a man can please me, I need to learn how to please a woman and how to be pleased by one.

Cain suddenly breaks the kiss, breathing heavily, then hooks my skirt up above my hips, while dropping to his knees. I gasp as he inserts a finger inside me, murmuring against what stepmother calls my 'clit'.

"I have first dibs, remember?"

I think it's all funny, the weird name and the guys' bickering, but I'm not laughing any more when Cain sucks on the swollen nub.

"Relax Dorran, she always has plenty to share. Don't you, Adrena?"

Basil asks in a voice as sweet as honey, and I moan in response, my nails digging into Cain's shoulders. His fingers and lips work miracles and tension begins to build inside my body. I let my eyes linger on the other two gorgeous men, and my heart skips a beat.

They couldn't be any more different, and yet, there is something about them that makes them the perfect trio. Cain with his light complexion and green eyes, Basil with his dark cropped hair that's shaved on the sides, and then Dorran, with his dark brown hair that's always secured tightly behind his back.

I have wondered many times what makes them so unique, and yet, so similar at the same time. It isn't the matching clothes, nor the constant stubble that darkens their chins. It isn't even the way they all love to worship me, and demand to be worshipped in return.

If I had to guess, I would say it's the passion and storm behind their eyes. They are the colours of the rainbow, and yet, they tell the same tale: a tale of hunters that saw too much and lived too little. I can't exactly say that they don't have experience in love though...

A sigh escapes me as Cain bites down on my clit, and I watch as both Basil and Dorran shed their leather trousers, their muscle-clad bodies only covered by their loose linen shirts now.

"Someone... could... see... us..."

I hiss between ragged breaths, and Dorran walks up to me, reaches behind me and grabs my hair, forcing my face towards him. I inhale sharply and he presses his demanding lips against mine, the motions of his tongue similar to those of Cain's.

He holds the back of my head firmly, while pinching and twisting a nipple, sending painful shivers down my spine. I moan again as I reach my first climax (another funny name my stepmother told me about - well, she *showed* me what it meant, to be precise), and both Cain and Dorran let me go. I pant with arousal.

"So... how do you want me?"

I ask, blushing. We are yet to discuss what they are craving most. Until now, I have been denying them the pleasure. Basil joins us and I smile at him.

"Get down on all fours. We will take turns today, seeing how you are still being mean and not letting us fuck you in the ass."

My cheeks burn with shame and embarrassment and I bite my lip. Cain rolls his eyes at Basil.

"Stop pressuring her. She will let us do it when she is ready."

I'm grateful for Cain's kindness, but my heart sinks when Dorran takes Basil's side:

"You know as well as we do that Clarise won't be pleased. Adrena's future husband will want her in every possible way, and if she doesn't let us teach her, she is in for a lot of pain and suffering."

I wince at his words, knowing that he is right. Cain sighs, giving in.

"I know you are right, but it isn't like she is getting married tomorrow. We still have time."

I know I only have a few seconds before they have a heated argument about me (or worse, they beat each other up, like many times in the past), so I clear my throat. Suddenly, all eyes turn back to me. I let out a ragged breath, almost too scared to say what I have to say, but I made up my mind already. I want them, in every way I can.

"I want you to teach me."

Cain opens his mouth then closes it again. Dorran tilts his head to the side, studying me with an expression I am not familiar with. Is he angry with me?

"Adrena, are you sure?"

He asks and I nod, then hold my head up high.

"I'm sure."

He shakes his head, while walking up to me.

"Get down on all fours. Now."

It's an order and I obey, shuddering. I can feel my nipples harden, and my flesh breaks out in tiny bumps. Dorran hikes my skirt up over my hips and puts a hand on my bare ass. Then, without any notice, he pushes his cock (another funny word made up by my stepmother) into my pussy. I cry out as his girth and length stretch me painfully, hands slipping on the wet grass. As a result, his cock slides in deeper, fully penetrating me. He says in a hushed, yet authoritative voice:

"Once you let us do it, there is no going back...We will want to take you in your butt every time we have sex, and most of the times all three of us will be fucking you at the same time. Is that what you really want?"

I gulp again, watching as both Basil and Cain walk up in front of me. Dutifully, I grab a cock in each hand, like I have done many times before. Panting, I reply:

"Maybe you could ease me into it? I mean, I don't think I will ever be ready..."

I bite my lower lip, and feel something hard and huge against my butthole (funny word number ten thousand). Trying to distract myself, unable to believe that this is finally happening, I run my hands up and down Basil's and Cain's cocks, while Dorran fucks me from behind.

"This might hurt a little."

Dorran says, then pushes something long and hard deep inside my ass.

~o~

Chapter 4

~o~

I close my eyes for a second, biting my lip to stop from screaming. Dorran keeps moving that thing in and out of my tight hole, and nothing works to ease the burning pain.

"A little?"

I hiss, and he suddenly stops, letting out a sigh. Unfortunately, he stops moving his cock inside me, too.

"I told you she isn't ready. Besides, you aren't doing it gently enough."

Cain says, pulling his cock away from me. If I wasn't still holding Basil's cock in the other hand, I would surely topple forward.

"Do you think you can do a better job?"

Dorran bites, then sighs again.

"I'm sorry, it's just... I want her so badly."

A tear rushes into my eyes. It's not like this is the first time I'm experiencing pain, so why can't I do this for them? Cain shakes his head, while walking up behind me. I can't see what he is doing, but I can feel his hand on my ass cheeks, pulling them apart gently. The wind tickles my now sore opening.

"Basil, bring the special flask."

I raise an eyebrow, but Basil nods, and I watch his delicious ass as he walks up to the horses and fetches a bluish-purple bottle, filled with a fluorescent liquid.

"What is that?"

I ask, half scared, half curious. Basil hands it over to Cain, and I glance back over my shoulder, watching him pour some of the liquid onto my cheeks, then slowly massaging it into my skin.

"Oh, that's cold and... uh..."

Suddenly, all colours come alive and dance in front of my eyes.

"Is that?"

I whisper, but I am unable to form a coherent sentence. The liquid soothes my skin, and when Cain works it around my butthole, the burning sensation goes away and is replaced by a delicious tingling.

"It's magic. A lavender-base potion to ease both your nerves and your pain, courtesy of Clarise."

Basil explains, while taking up his previous position in front of me. I dutifully grab his cock once more, rubbing it up and down.

"How does it feel now?"

Cain asks, before pouring some of the liquid onto Dorran's cock, too. The liquid is dripping into my pussy, making me instantly open up and tingle inside.

"It's weird, but I like it. And it doesn't hurt any more."

Dorran's strained voice makes me shudder:

"About time. I can barely hold back in here. You are too damn tight, Adrena, as always."

My cheeks burn once again, and when Dorran playfully slaps my ass, my *other* cheeks begin to burn as well. he starts moving inside me at the same time, and I scream out in pure pleasure.

"In the name of all the Gods, what the hell is... ah.... oh..."

Basil takes this as an opportunity to push his hard member between my parted lips, and I am not complaining. The magic potion is giving me unearthly sensations I never knew existed. I lick the tip, and Basil groans, grabbing my ebony curls and twisting them around his wrist.

"Be a good girl and go down deeper."

He whispers, but before I could do as he asked, he has already pulled me down the length of him. I choke a little, my coughing getting lost around his thick shaft.

"Maybe we should have made her drink some of the potion, eh? You are too big for her."

Cain says in concern, but Dorran increases his pace and I moan, my throat automatically easing up.

"Nonsense. You can go all the way down, can't you, Adrena?"

Basil purrs, stroking my hair. I know I don't have anything to prove, but I want to. Closing my eyes and taking a deep breath, I inch closer to the base where his tight balls are (funny word number ten thousand and one - sometimes I feel like a walking dictionary).

Basil gasps, grabbing my hair tighter, and by doing so, he pushes me deeper onto his cock. Tears swell in my eyes, and I ease back up a bit, and because he seems to be enjoying that, I repeat the movement.

"Hurry up, Cain, because I wasn't kidding when I said I'm about to cum."

Dorran hisses behind me, pushing faster and harder into my pussy. It feels like he is deeper than ever before, but it doesn't hurt. In fact, the tension building within my core is so unique and intense that I can hardly breathe (I know that Basil's cock has something to do with that, too, but still).

"Fine. Adrena, I will now open your asshole up with my fingers, then push one inside to begin with. Give me a sign if it hurts too much and I will stop."

I mumble my approval against Basil's cock, making him hiss.

"Can you not do that, man? Otherwise I will be in the same predicament as Dorran."

Cain lets out a sigh, probably shaking his head at the other two, before doing what he said he would. This time, when the tip of his finger enters my tight asshole, I flinch a little, expecting a lot of pain and burning, but to my surprise, his finger slides in easily, and it doesn't hurt at all. The tingling is there, warming my insides, and there is a weird pleasure, that's on the brink of being uncomfortable, but I can deal with that.

"Wow, that shit really helped."

Dorran says, then growls as I feel the muscles in my pussy clench around his shaft when Cain pulls his finger out of my ass completely, then pushes it back again.

"Jeez, she is even tighter then before..."

Dorran hisses, grabbing onto my ass. It's weird how Cain's finger is still inside, and I am being pleasured by two of the hunters, while I'm pleasuring the third one. Feeling bold all of a sudden I reach out and grab Basil's balls in my right hand, balancing myself on his hips with my left.

"And she is way bolder than before."

Basil adds in a hushed voice, then caresses my cheek:

"You certainly know how to... Oh, Gods..."

I chuckle around his cock, squeezing his balls tighter. Dorran laughs behind me, although his laughter is strained as well.

"Cain, I think she needs to be taught another lesson. She is more than ready."

Cain chuckles himself, surprising me. He is always the serious one out of them three. He pulls his finger out of my ass, and Dorran ceases his movements inside my pussy. Even Basil makes sure that my lips disconnect from his cock.

"No, she isn't ready for that yet, trust me. But I can do something else."

I glance back in time to watch him place two fingers against my asshole, massaging gently. I moan, feeling the tingles open me up. Suddenly, Dorran pulls out completely. I look at him questioningly, but he shrugs.

"You need to experience this fully and without distractions."

I shake my head.

"But what about you guys?"

I ask, glancing from basil to Dorran. Basil strokes my cheeks once again.

"Don't worry, Adrena. Once Cain opened you up, we will all fuck you senseless."

My breath hitches and Dorran nods, watching as Cain plays with my ass.

"Trust me, you will wish you never asked us to teach you."

I want to say something, but Cain shoots Dorran and Basil a warning glance.

"That's enough. Both of you. After this, no more butt stuff for today. You can only claim her pussy, is that clear?"

Dorran huffs and crosses his arms in front of his chest, but because Cain stops his teasing and glares at him, he simply shrugs.

"As you wish. But do hurry up before I can't control myself."

Cain rolls his eyes, then turns his attention back to my ass. Basil's and Dorran's eyes linger there, too, and I gasp.
This is going to be a long and exciting day for sure...

~o~

Chapter 5

~o~

When I finally wake up, my mind is on fire and my wound burns. But I'm alive. Dread washes over me as I sit up, glancing at the wound, only to frown. Instead of a gash oozing dark green liquid, there is but a tiny pink scar, barely visible. I furrow my brows further when I notice that I'm feeling warm and cosy, with something soft underneath and around me.

I blink a few times, so my eyes can adjust to the darkness, and a gasp leaves my lips as three pairs of eyes stare at me with blank expressions.

"Hello, Adrena."

Cain says, his normally caring voice cold as ice. I gulp down my fear, considering the fact that I might still be dreaming, even though deep down I know I'm not. This is real. They found me, and I'm not dead, which means that I'm screwed. Basil steps forward and I crawl backwards, the thick furs falling off my body as I move. Basil frowns.

"Where did she get those furs from?"

He asks, turning to Cain. he shrugs. Dorran huffs, pushing past him and scooping me up in his arms, furs and all. I try to protest, but I'm way too weak, and he is too damn strong. The smell of leather, the one that aroused me so many times before is trying to do its job once again, but I push the thought aside. I'm not going to offer myself up in order to save myself.

I might have loved them once, but they are no longer those people. Only the Gods know what kind of magic spell the evil queen put them under.

"It doesn't matter. Let's go."

Panic rises within me as Dorran holds me tight, lifting me off the ground. I push against his chest, but its no use. I refuse to give up though.

"Easy. I don't want to hurt you yet."

He whispers, sending a shiver down my spine.

"Where... where are you taking me?"

I ask, voice trembling with fear. Dorran glances at Cain, and when he nods, Dorran turns back to me and says, tucking a curl behind my ear:

"Somewhere safe - for now."

I open my mouth to say something, but no words leave my lips. My mind goes completely blank, too. Did he really say what I think he said?

"But the arrows..."

I mumble, baffled.

"They missed you, didn't they?"

Cain's impatient voice makes me lose interest in asking any more questions. I don't tell them that one of them didn't. It doesn't make sense. None of it does. I should be dead. They should be trying to kill me and...

"Guys, we need to hurry. She is coming."

Basil says in an urgent tone, and suddenly they are all running and I'm tucked so deep into the furs that I can't see or hear much. All there is is Dorran's heartbeat and my own ragged breathing. Where the hell are they taking me?

And more importantly: what the hell do they want with me?

More books in the Reverse Harem Chronicles are on their way.

Please visit my website www.timeatokes.com to sign up for my newsletter, and I would really appreciate it if you let me know what you thought about this short story.

Thanks a lot!

~o~

A tempting taste of other, bite-size erotica, from the naughty pen of Timea Tokes:

~o~

DOMINATED BY BILLIONAIRES
(SAMPLE)

One hour, a cold shower and hundred pages later, I can proudly say that my doubts have been cleared. I have the whole night laid out in front of me, and I must admit, the prospect of doing this is beginning to sound tempting once again. And it sounds easy. Not too easy for it not to be true though. I check myself in the mirror one last time before heading out into the lobby.

Black strapless dress: check. Black stilettos: check. No panties: check. Diamond earrings: check. According to the papers, the earrings are a little curtesy from Alec for all my troubles. I raised an eyebrow at that, especially considering the amount he is paying me, but I won't look a gift horse in the mouth, at least not tonight. And, if he does turn out to be a serial killer, I might even enjoy the last bit of luxury I'm given.

A sigh escapes me as I run my hand down the length of the velvety fabric. I have never worn something so intricate or something that would feel so amazing on my skin. The heels are a bit high, but the last half an hour provided enough practice. I run a comb through my hair once more, just to make sure, and I apply the fruity perfume Alec left on the side table. I must admit that he has an exquisite taste.

It's weird how quickly time flies between that moment and the one where I get into the black limo. And then, time suddenly stops again when I glance into the most beautiful brown pair of eyes I've ever seen. Well, three pairs, to be precise.

Just like in an action movie, when you see the hero in slow motion, kicking ass, I'm seeing the three guys in slow motion, too. But it might even be that nobody speaks for minutes, and that's why I have the chance to ogle them, I wouldn't know. All I know is that I could have done worse. Way worse.

Okay, suit number one is adorable, looking a bit like David Beckham, with his dirty blond side-cut, midnight blue suit, white shirt and blue tie. He reaches up to fix said tie the same way as Beckham does in one of his commercials, and I'm sold.

My eyes shift on their own accord to suit number two. I don't think I'm doing this in invisible mode, it's more likely that they are simply being polite about it. But either way, suit number two is delicious, too. He is clearly the rebel one, with a stripy suit, pink shirt and a matching stripy tie. He has a black moustache, but even that looks mischievous and misbehaving. His hair is an unruly black, further confirming my theory.

And of course, I am saving the best for last: suit number three, although he deserves to be mentioned before everyone else. Part of me is hoping that he has the magic voice, too. I'm utterly surprised that he is my favourite, purely because he doesn't have hair at all. I mean, his head is completely bald, and apart from a pair of charcoal eyebrows that sport a silver hoop, there is no hair on the guy. Well, on his face, at least.

His suit is crisp and white, and although I never learnt psychology, I can tell that he knows how to take control of the situation. The funny thing is that all three of them have brown eyes, at least something less comical and more human. I always thought brown eyes were dull, but I take that back now. Caramel, hazel, chestnut, you name it. Those three pairs of eyes change shades like someone changes underwear, and all of them are sexy as hell.

I gulp, finally realising that I'm staring. Suit number three clears his throat and my cheeks burn with shame. Yes, he is my guy, the one who bought me. And yes, I just made a fool of myself, confirming that I would do this for free, too, if given the chance.

'Olivia, it's lovely to meet you.'

He says, the velvety smooth voice professional, yet his mocha eyes assessing me coolly. I nod at all three of them, smiling sweetly.

'Hello to you, too. Here. I've signed on the dotted line, so I guess I'm yours for the night.'

I sound so cheesy, and I know myself that I'm asking for it. But there is no way I'm not playing them (and hopefully defeating them) in their own game. Alec glances at the signature, then shakes his head. I raise an eyebrow as his chocolate-coloured pair pierces into mine.

'I understand you thought you could get away with using a fake name. And that's okay, we won't use that against you. But here's the deal.'

I gulp, realising that I've been caught. I thought if I signed under the fake name, I could get out anytime. But no, I don't have that luxury. I keep forgetting that people with money can do whatever they like and can find out as much information about anyone as they want. They know no limits. How could I pretend to outsmart them?

~o~

Dominated
By
Billionaires
A Reverse Harem Why Choose
Billionaire BDSM
Romance Collection
Timea Tokes

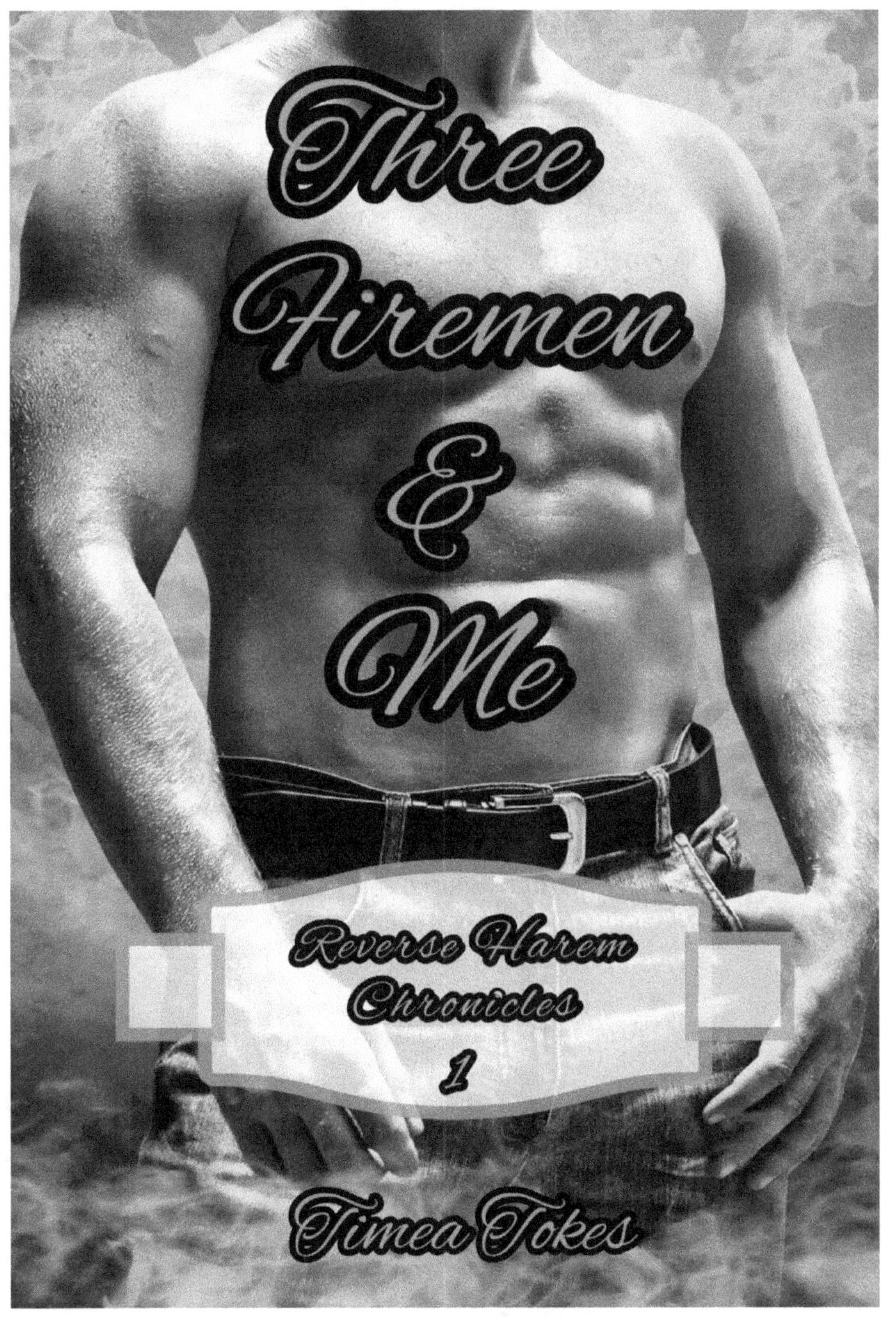
Three
Firemen
&
Me
Reverse Harem
Chronicles
1
Timea Tokes

<u>Other Books by Timea Tokes:</u>

<u>Reverse Harem Chronicles:</u>
Three Firemen & Me 1-2
Three Policemen & Me 1-2
Three Billionaires & Me 1-3
Dominated by my Neighbours 1-5 **(NEW)**

<u>Reverse Harem Fairy Tales:</u>
Kiss & Tell Tail 1-5
Snow White Desire **(NEW)**

<u>BDSM Billionaire:</u>
Watched **(NEW)**

<u>Dominant Women:</u>
Domina By Accident

<u>Holiday Romance:</u>
Screwing Miss Scrooge
Mistletoe Boss
Dating The Author (Why Choose)
My Hitch-Hiking Valentine
The Bucket List 1-2
Truth or Dare?
Dominating Magic 1-3

<u>Gay:</u>
The Stranger

<u>Paranormal Romance:</u>
Her First And Last Secret Admirer

<u>Other BDSM Romance:</u>
A Special Cup of Coffee – Pain and Pleasure
Stuck & Shared
Squirm Under My Watch
How About the Rooftop?
Don't Make A Sound
Seducing the Plumber 1-2
The Escort's Taxi ride 1-3
The Good Neighbor 1-5
Forgotten
Blue Highlights

<u>Collections of Short Stories:</u>
Claim Me This Winter
Love Me This Year
Dominated By Billionaires
Dominated by Strangers 1
Dominated by Strangers 2
Dominated by Men in Uniforms
Dominating the Escort
Dominating Magic 1-3
Kiss and Tell Tail 1-5
You Had Me At Kinky
You Had Me At Steamy
You Had Me At Rough

Coming Soon:

Dominated By My Neighbours 4 (2021)
Caught (BDSM Billionaire 2) (2021)
Snow White Longing (2021)
Domina by Choice (Domina Diaries 2) 2021

Follow Timea Tokes on:

Amazon @timea_tokes

Twitter @timea_tokes

Facebook @herfirstsecret

Goodreads @timea_tokes

Sign up to her newsletter, and have a look at her blog for more bite-size erotica, paranormal romance, reviews and more:

www.timeatokes.com

<u>Note from the Author, Timea Tokes:</u>

~o~

My dear, lovely Reader, thank you for taking the time to read my story! I really hope you enjoyed it as much as I did writing it. As always, your feedback is highly valued and much appreciated.

Please do take the time to scroll to the end of the book and leave a review. It would mean the World to me!

And remember, this story is all about your pleasure.

On the next page, you can learn a bit more about me and why I write, but you will also find author interviews (and much more) on my website.

~o~

ABOUT THE AUTHOR

~o~

I have been writing short stories and poems since a young age, but my ultimate goal was creating a novel. Or a series, rather. Now, with my four paranormal romance novels published, as well as more than 30 erotica titles under my belt, , I think I can say that it came true - but this only fuels my desire to write more. After all, we are allowed to dream the same dream (over and over again) - and that's exactly what I'm planning to do :)

I enjoy helping people in any way possible, and I really hope that my books will prove to be inspirational in a way. Whether readers are looking for a swift (and steamy) erotic story, or a paranormal romance, I want them to associate themselves with my characters and realize stuff about themselves in the process.

Yes, even the bad things. Because, in life, there is no black and white, only colors. Therefore, I don't think any of my characters are either good or bad, but rather a little bit of both.

Aren't we all?

Well, if you never had guilty thoughts, never had any self-confidence issues, or if you never wanted something (or someone) who belonged to someone else, then probably my books won't be for you. But, who knows, I might be able to show you a different perspective. I like to experiment with different genres, and new concepts and ideas.

I really enjoy learning as much as I can about people, what makes them tick (and live, laugh, cry, and sigh). In fact, I think our World (and those beyond) are so diverse, ten thousand lifetimes wouldn't be enough to explore it all. But one thing I truly believe in: those who belong in your life will find a way there. Therefore my stories are usually based on chance encounters and ordinary events that take an unexpected turn.

Like a blind date on Valentine's day, or a haircut, or a new job. Who says you can't meet someone 'accidentally'; while going to the hairdresser, someone you lost contact with 500 years ago? Trust me, you can. You just need to brace every day (and every book) with open eyes - and an open heart.

Just remember: my stories are all about you, and you alone. If they capture your attention (and your heart), then I've done my 'job'. I regularly try to release new content, both on Amazon and my blog. Please feel free to have a look, and sign up to my newsletter.

And, just so you know: I care about your opinion, very much so. Whether you liked my work or you didn't, I would be honored if you let me know what it meant for you. It would mean the world to me!

~o~

1. *When did you create your first erotica story, and what was it about?*

Well, my first story wasn't fully erotica, more a romance story. In fact, I never thought that one day I would write anything steamy. Not at all. I was shy, and grew up in an environment, where everything was taboo. Sharing my views on sex with anyone, let alone write about it? No way...

And yet, I soon had to realize that writing romantic stories couldn't happen without the couple getting it on eventually. Especially because the first four books series I created was about the same characters, and they are 100 pages each (which is a lot to go without including a sex scene every now and again). I must admit, I delayed the inevitable for as long as I could, just to realize later how much I enjoyed writing about sex.

Although my first attempts were very timid indeed, I tried to avoid being too explicit or descriptive. I concentrated on the romantic and paranormal aspect of it (the main characters dream about each other, and somehow when I was writing about the dreams, they gave me courage to be a bit braver).

But it wasn't until I started writing my erotic short stories in 2015, when I started to experiment. Well, if you have a look at 'The Good Neighbour', you can see how my explicitness and mood changed throughout the series.

I think I can say that this was the very first fully erotic story I created, fulfilling one of my secret fantasies (no, I don't have a hot neighbour, or at least I don't think I have, but the idea always fascinated me).

2. *What (or who) inspired you to start writing erotica?*

My own lack of courage, if I'm honest. All my friends were so open about their relationships and their fantasies, so I thought:

"Why do I have to be this way, when I want to explore everything that's out there?"

And as I have always enjoyed writing, I decided to try it out on paper. It started as a therapy I prescribed for myself, and then it escalated, taking me to places I never thought I would visit. I must say that I'm really glad I gave in to temptation.

3. *What do you find most challenging when writing these stories?*

To let them go when I finish writing them. I believe that it isn't possible, especially when I create a longer story. The characters, the feelings stay with me long after, as they become part of me for at least a little while.

Another aspect of it is that I keep thinking about what others read into them, and whether they convey their meaning in a way that I intended them to. But, just like when you give birth to a child, when writing a story as well you need to give it space after some time.

I once read a quotation (not sure where, or who said it, but it made me smile and I could definitely relate):

"I met the man of my dreams last night.. in chapter five..." *Sigh*

4. *Do you write in other genres, and if yes, then would you consider mixing them with erotica?*

Yes, and not sure. I ghost-write for a living, as well as create my own stories, which include romance, horror, thriller, fantasy, crime and more, but I'm not sure it would feel right to mix them with erotica. Mind that, I have had some strange requests that were a mixture, like fetish-horror, but it didn't actually include erotica. I suppose it could have, as it was about a foot fetish, which seems to be quite popular. Oh well, another thing to look at in the future :)

My favourite ones are psychological thrillers though, so I could probably turn one of those into erotica, but at the moment I'm thinking of a transition, rather than a mix. So, for example it would start as a thriller, but have a sexual ending. Hmm...

5. *Have you written any stories that were inspired by real life events?*

Yes. In fact, my very first story, 'Her First and Last Secret Admirer' (the four books I mentioned earlier) started with an actual recurring medieval dream, which I then implemented into the plot, creating a story and background for it. If it wasn't for that urge to put the whole thing into writing, I probably would never have picked up the courage to write at all. Now it is both in print and on Kindle, so I guess it was a nice bargain :)

I think that writing about real events, twisting them a little, but still keeping them close to your heart is an important process.

Also, that way you can relive those events over and over again, and others will keep guessing what was the real part in it.

Strangely enough, it adds to its mystery (and excitement, of course)...

6. *What is your speciality and why?*

I would say it's mixing the past with the present. I'm not an expert, but I also love to keep up the suspense until the end. Although this doesn't always come through in my erotic stories, as they are linear, but in my paranormal romance books, I draw a parallel between what happened 500 years ago and what's happening right now. It's difficult to explain without revealing the plot itself, but I do love to play with the mind of the reader, if you know what I mean.

7. *Are there any topics you don`t like writing about?*

Now? Not really. If you asked me a few years ago, I would have said everything that involves sex ;)

I guess I just realized that I shouldn't say no, just because I don't know how something feels. If I don't try it, I will never know... If I'm not familiar with a topic, then I do my research, but not too many things scare me nowadays (without wanting to sound weird or vain).

8. *Do you have any tips / warnings for newbie erotica writers?*

Follow your dreams. You will get some ugly feedback (or none at all), but that doesn't mean that your work isn't appreciated. Don't take them personally, but accept them, so that they can serve as stepping stones, helping you improve your writing. We all make mistakes; that's what makes us human.

Personally, I couldn't wait to grab a physical copy of my books, and that made up for whatever negativity I got (but luckily it has only been minor stuff so far).

So, if you are thinking about writing, or if you already have a story or two, try to make them into a book, no matter how tiny it is. Trust me, as soon as you have it on your shelf, you will become a different person.

9. *What is your favourite season and why?*

Spring, because that's when everything comes to life. I just love to watch the flowers blossom and the world wake up from its winter slumber. I always feel like I'm reborn myself every time springs comes (I know, I'm a hopeless romantic).